Billibonk
& the
Thorn Patch

Billibonk & the thorn Patch

Philip Ramsey

Illustrated by Robin Runci Mazo
and Madaleen Pulsifer

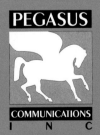

PEGASUS COMMUNICATIONS, INC.   CAMBRIDGE

Billibonk and the Thorn Patch by Philip Ramsey
Copyright © 1997 by Philip Ramsey
Art © Robin Runci Mazo and Madaleen Pulsifer

Library of Congress Cataloging-in-Publication Data
Ramsey, Philip.
Billibonk and the thorn patch / Philip Ramsey ; art by Robin Runci Mazo and Madaleen
Pulsifer
ISBN 1-883823-09-9
l. Jungle animals—Fiction. 2. Problem solving—Fiction. 3. Fables, International.
I. Mazo, Robin Runci, and Pulsifer, Madaleen II. Title.
PS3568.A471B55 1996
813'.54—dc21   96-39253
                                                      CIP

Acquisitions editor: Kellie Wardman O'Reilly
Project editor: Lauren Johnson
Design, hand lettering, and production: Judy Walker
Proofreader: Joy Sobeck

♻ Printed on recycled paper.
Printed in the United States of America.
First edition

PEGASUS
COMMUNICATIONS
I N C

http://www.pegasuscom.com

Dedicated To

my wonderful children,

Alexandra and Nicholas.

Thanks for all your help

with the story.

Contents

Part One

The Thorn Patch

The jungle of Knith was home to a vast array of birds, animals, plants, and flowers. The many sizes, shapes, and colors of the jungle's creatures and vegetation made Knith a beautiful place. Every day and night, the jungle was filled with the sounds of monkeys screeching, mice rustling and squeaking, elephants trumpeting. And because each animal was unique in how it reasoned and behaved, the jungle was full of stories. . . .

The most fascinating stories usually involved mice, for they were the smartest of Knith's inhabitants, and they were intensely curious about everything. Perhaps they were smart because they were so small. They were not strong or fierce, so to get other animals to listen to them, the mice had to be clever.

The elephants, on the other hand, were not considered clever at all. Rather than thinking about things, they preferred to spend their time eating, lying in the sun, and taking an occasional swim.

All the other animals in the jungle agreed that elephants were so big they could get away with tremendous blunders. Of course, the elephants did not think these "blunders" were their fault; it just seemed to them that they had a lot of bad luck.

One of the "unluckiest" elephants was Billibonk. Tall, even for an elephant, Billibonk had the habit of curling the end of his trunk upward as he walked. This trick kept his sensitive trunk away from his heavy feet, *and* it helped him sniff out his favorite foods: yakka-yakka leaves. Like many elephants, Billibonk often walked into things, usually while eating. Elephants have enormous appetites and, in the jungle, they eat vast quantities of leaves. Sadly, they have not learned how to look up at the leaves and down at their feet at the same time. They do, however, have very thick skin, so the bangs and scratches they get are usually not too bad.[1]

On this particular day, with his head in the air, eyes searching for fresh, new leaves, Billibonk accidentally walked into the biggest patch of thorns in the jungle.

---

[1] Elephants are sometimes called "pachyderms," which means "thick skins." Mice, though, prefer to call them "pachycraniums," meaning "thick heads." Mice can be very rude.

Billibonk became aware of his mistake (or, as he would say, his "bad luck") when a stabbing pain shot through his foot. Trumpeting loudly, he leapt in the air, and then came crashing down, bottom first, on the thorns.

Billibonk burst into tears. As he cried, huge sobs shook his whole body. Each time he shook, his bottom bounced on the thorns, making him cry even more loudly. With every second, Billibonk's misery worsened. The more he cried, the more he shook. The more he shook, the more it hurt. And the more it hurt, the more he cried. Soon the whole jungle could hear him.

Frankl, one of the many mice who lived among the thorns, had been awakened by the thump of Billibonk's fall. Frankl was an ordinary-looking mouse in most respects. What set him apart from other mice was his intense fascination with everything about the jungle. He loved to find out why things happened the way they did. His intelligent eyes sparkling, he decided to investigate the strange noise.

As the elephant's howls grew in volume, Frankl climbed a high thorn bush close to Billibonk's ear. Sucking in a deep breath, he yelled, "Hey, elephant!"[2]

Frankl's yell surprised Billibonk—mice do not usually get so close to an elephant's ear—and, abruptly, he stopped his wailing. When he stopped crying, he also stopped shaking. As he stopped shaking, the sharp pain of the thorns turned into a dull ache.

Sniffling, he turned to look for the source of the yell. Standing on a branch, staring at him, was a bright-eyed little mouse!

"It looks like you have a problem, elephant," Frankl said.

"I do. My name is Billibonk, and my bottom is sore."

"That's probably because you are sitting on thorns," said Frankl. "Seems to me you'd better get up and walk out of there."

Billibonk thought about this for a moment. "But that'll hurt!" he protested, and then he started crying again; crying, shaking, hurting, and crying some more until Frankl's ears were ringing.

---

[2] This is the usual form of greeting used in the jungle. It is not considered at all impolite.

Once more Frankl yelled, "Hey, elephant!" and once again it did the trick. Billibonk stopped sobbing.

Frankl, trying to be as kind as he could, said, "Billibonk. I don't want to make you cry again—I know how much it hurts you. But you can't stay where you are, unless you don't mind eating thorns."

Billibonk really did not want to move, so he thought for a minute about eating thorns. If they felt so bad on his outside, he reasoned, they would probably hurt even more on his inside.

With a sob, Billibonk heaved himself upright. He closed his eyes, gritted his tusks, and started staggering back the way he had come. Once again the thorns jabbed into his feet. Up into the air he jumped. But this time when he crashed down, he managed to land outside the thorn patch.

Frankl was impressed with the elephant's effort. He climbed down from his perch and scurried over to where Billibonk was sprawled. Patting him on one of his massive toenails, he said, "Billibonk, that took real courage. You're quite an elephant."

Billibonk began to feel rather pleased with himself. Picking himself up, he said, "Thanks, mouse!" Then he looked up at the jungle canopy and spotted a fresh clump of yakka-yakka leaves. With his head in the air, he stomped off toward them. "Those leaves will make a nice reward for my courage," he thought to himself.

From all around the jungle floor came a chorus of little voices yelling, "Hey, elephant!" Billibonk stopped in his tracks. He looked down. He had been about to step back into the thorn patch!

Billibonk blushed a little and muttered, "Now that would've really been bad luck." He set off again, this time taking care to avoid the thorn patch.

Elephants Thinking

When something goes wrong for an elephant, usually the elephant decides, "That was bad luck," and then forgets about it. Billibonk, however, kept thinking about the mouse who had helped him out of the thorn patch. The mouse had been so clever. Could an elephant ever think that well?

Billibonk decided to try. He decided to think about thorn patches and how to stay out of them. This was something new to Billibonk, so he did his thinking in short spells, usually during the contented time after eating, when his stomach was full. In a few days, Billibonk had "The Idea." It was an idea he knew he had to share with the other elephants.

So he waited until that evening, after the herd had bathed in the swimming hole. As the elephants relaxed together, Billibonk shyly spoke up. "Excuse me, everyone. I . . . I have an idea."

This was such an unusual thing for an elephant to say that the herd all immediately pricked up their ears. The only sound was the rustling of leaves, caused by the breeze created by so many elephant ears being pricked. Jawoody, a matriarch of the herd, was especially interested. She was older than most of the others. Her wrinkles were deeper and her tusks more yellowed, and everyone respected her opinion. She had a deep curiosity about anything new, and finally demanded, "Well, what is it?"

Clearing his throat, Billibonk began. "The other day, I had some very bad luck. I got stuck in a patch of thorns. My bottom was so sore that it still hurts to sit down. I'm sure that many of you have had bad luck with thorns, too." At this, a few of the gathered elephants snorted in an agreeing way. "Maybe we should think about clearing all the thorns out of the jungle," Billibonk suggested.

The herd silently considered this idea. Finally Honka announced, "I hate thorns." Honka was enormous—the largest elephant in the herd. In fact, his head was so big the edges of his ears were ragged from being slapped against the trees that line narrow jungle paths. Nodding his huge head, he complained, "Thorns are the worst thing about this jungle. Sometimes there are really big patches right under the nicest yakka-yakka trees." Other elephants realized that this was true.[3]

Then Jawoody spoke. "What a great idea! And I'm so glad an elephant had it. Clearing the thorns from this jungle will show everyone how clever elephants can be."

At this the herd began stamping and trumpeting their approval. Even those who had started worrying about how much work clearing the thorns would be forgot their concerns and joined in the excited noise-making.

When the clamor finally died down, Jawoody said, "If we're going to show those short-snouts[4] how clever we are, we'll have to do this properly. We need a plan."

"Before we plan, shouldn't we find out where all the thorn patches are in the jungle?" asked Billibonk.

"Excellent thinking," said Jawoody. "Let's start with a survey of the jungle. We begin tomorrow, after breakfast."

---

[3] It did not occur to Honka—or any of the others—that yakka-yakka trees surrounded by thorn patches grow well because the thorns keep the elephants away from the trees.

[4] This is a rather rude name used by elephants when they talk about other animals in the jungle.

CHAPTER THREE

The Thorn Bush Survey

After breakfast the next morning, the survey began. At first the entire herd set off to survey the same thorn patch, but soon they were better organized. They spread out, covering different parts of the jungle.

Other animals watched with great fascination and wonderment. None of them had ever before seen elephants so interested in anything except eating.

One inquisitive mouse named Yollanda observed as Honka paced out the distance around her thorn patch and then started counting.

As Honka passed near her, Yollanda called out, "Hey, elephant. What are you doing?"

Honka replied, "Keep quiet, short-snout. You nearly made me lose count."

"Lose count of what?"

"Of the thorn bushes in this patch," said Honka.

"Why on earth would you want to count thorn bushes?" asked Yollanda.

"Because," said Honka proudly, "we elephants are going to clear all the thorn patches in this jungle."

"I can't believe it! Not even elephants would want to do *that*," gasped Yollanda.

"What do you mean? Getting rid of the thorns is a brilliant idea!"

"Have you thought about the mice and birds and insects who live in the thorn patches? You'll be ruining our homes!" said Yollanda.

"Oh. We didn't think of that. What bad luck for you short-snouts."

"Bad luck! This isn't bad luck! It's a bad decision!"

Honka got angry. "This is a wonderful decision. All the herd agrees.[5] And anyway, living in thorns is what is really stupid. Who would want to live in things that hurt?"

"They don't hurt *us!*" shouted Yollanda. "But they do hurt anyone who tries to walk on our homes. *That's* why we live here."

"Well, if you're so clever, you won't have trouble finding somewhere else to live," snorted Honka, and he stomped off toward the watering hole.

---

[5] Elephants believe that if they all agree about something, then it must be true. They also think that it is rather offensive to disagree with one another. These two ideas, when put together, sometimes lead elephants to believe the strangest things.

Mice in Action

Thorn patches are made up of individual thorn bushes. From the outside, a patch looks like it has thorns everywhere. In fact, as a thorn bush grows, natural spaces are created around its base, under its branches. Small animals can build their homes in these spaces. Sometimes, because of the way several bushes grow together, an extra-large space is created. Mice call these big spaces "chambers."

As word of the elephants' plan spread quickly among the mice, an emergency meeting of the Mouse Council was called that evening, to take place within one of the largest thorn-patch chambers in the jungle. Mice from all over Knith gathered at the Council thorn patch to discuss the problem.

Ragou, the head of the Mouse Council, called for silence, and addressed the group. "We are here to discuss a dangerous situation," he announced. "As you will know by now, the elephants are planning to clear all the thorns out of the jungle. We should decide whether we need to do anything, and if so, what."

An excitable young mouse named Bekk jumped to his feet. "What do you mean 'if'? Of *course* we have to do something; these pachycraniums want to destroy our homes!"

Frankl—who usually stayed calm even in tense situations—raised his hand to speak. "Perhaps I can respond to that, Ragou. Dangers of all sorts have come and gone over the years, and we mice have learned from them. One thing we've learned is that we don't have to jump at every danger. Sometimes a problem goes away by itself. These elephants may never get around to pulling up a single thorn bush. Or they might start, but then get tired out."

"Well spoken, Frankl," said Ragou. Then noticing a hand waving toward the back of the clearing, he asked, "Yes, Yollanda?"

"I have spoken to one of these elephants, and I think we have to act," Yollanda stated. "The elephants think that clearing the thorns will prove that they're brilliant. And they're so big, they could clear a thorn patch in no time. They may tire out, but I don't want them to get tired while ruining *my* home!"[6]

---

[6] Unlike elephants, mice have a long history of openly disagreeing with one another when talking about important matters. Usually this happens without anyone becoming upset. Sometimes, though, feelings get hurt when a mouse forgets that the disagreement is about ideas and not about friendship.

Around the chamber, mice squeaked their agreement. Even Frankl nodded while he thought about the damage an excited elephant could do to a thorn patch.

"We seem to agree that something has to be done," said Ragou. "Does anyone have any ideas?"

"Well," said Frankl, "we could try teaching them about the rest of the animals in the jungle. If they knew how many birds and animals live in the thorns, maybe they'd think again about their plan."

"I tried talking to one," said Yollanda "but it was a complete waste of time. They won't listen. And even if they did, we can't afford the time to teach them. They'll be wrecking our homes tomorrow!"

"Maybe we could get them busy doing something else," called out one of the Council members. "We could set a couple of yakka-yakka trees on fire, and they'd be so busy putting out the fire they might forget about the thorns."

"We are not going to stop the elephants from ruining the jungle by ruining it ourselves!" said Ragou. "But your idea might help others to think of more ideas. Let's all take a moment to think of a practical way to solve this problem."

For several minutes, the mice silently considered the situation from all angles.[7]

Finally Ragou asked, "Does anyone have further thoughts?"

"I have," said one of the older mice. "The idea about the fire got me thinking that we could scare the elephants—but in a way that doesn't cause any damage. What if we told them that something horrible lived in the thorns? That would get their trunks in a knot!"

"I'm not sure," said Frankl. "That might stop them from clearing the thorns, but it doesn't get at the real problem. These elephants think they're the only important animals in the jungle. If they don't change that idea, they'll just keep on coming up with these dangerous schemes."

"Oh, come on, Frankl," said Yollanda. "We've already decided that trying to

---

[7] Mice often set aside time during their meetings to reflect on what others have said. In this way, they find new ways to look at old problems.

teach them just won't work. Scaring them will be fun. Haven't you ever wanted to see an elephant jump out of its baggy old skin?"

The mice rolled about on the ground, squeaking and cackling at the thought of a skinless elephant; all except for Frankl, who was blushing to the ends of his whiskers.

When the mice finally quieted down, Ragou said, "Well, then, we need a plan for scaring these elephants. We have to be ready for tomorrow." With that, the mice set about scheming. In the morning, they decided, the elephants would be in for a shock.

The Great Fright

As the sun rose the next morning, the jungle buzzed with activity. The birds were singing in chorus, and the elephants and mice busied themselves for an important day. The elephants had chosen a patch of thorns closest to the watering hole as the place to begin clearing.

The mice had actually expected them to start at this particular patch. It was close to the watering hole, it backed onto a clearing in which the herd could work, and it had a large, especially luscious yakka-yakka tree growing above it. The mice were ready!

As Jawoody led the elephant herd toward the patch, she was met by a sleek, dark mouse named Nettie. Nettie had been chosen for this part of the plan because of her acting skills and her loud voice. "Excuse me, mighty elephant," Nettie called. "You had better be careful. So many elephants walking this way could wake up the Thorn Monster!"

"Thorn Monster?" rumbled Jawoody. "What Thorn Monster?"

"You don't live in the thorns, so I suppose you've never seen it," replied Nettie. "Thorn Monsters live at the bottom of thorn patches. They like it there because it's quiet and they sleep a lot, and no one complains about their terrible smell. But when they wake up, they grab at whatever it is that woke them. Thorn Monsters are horrible."

"But *you* live in the thorns," said Jawoody. "Why doesn't the Thorn Monster scare *you?*"

Nettie, thinking fast, added to her story. "We're so small and quiet that Thorn Monsters don't mind us. And we keep the Thorn Monsters happy by dancing for them at each full moon and giving them gifts of flowers. Flowers cover their smell, you know."

The elephant herd began to shuffle their feet anxiously. Billibonk spoke up: "Well, I don't believe in these Thorn Monsters. You made them up."

"Oh, they are real. If you're careful, you can smell the one in this thorn patch. But be careful not to wake it up. Of course, you don't have to smell it if you're scared."

"I'm not scared," said Billibonk, though he shifted his weight back and forth nervously. "*I'll* smell it!"

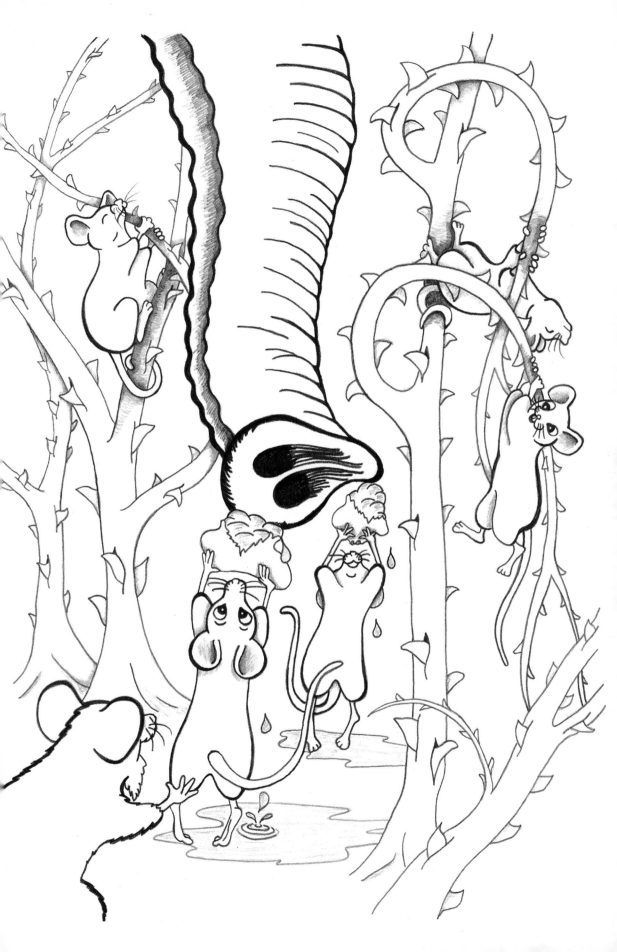

Scrambling up onto a bush, Nettie pointed to a gap in the thorns and said, "Slide your trunk down into this hole, and take a deep breath."

Inside the thorn patch, Ragou and a large group of mice waited. Two teams of mice held back the springy thorn branches, waiting for Ragou's signal. Another team waited lower down in the thorns, by a pile of crushed "stink-plant" berries.

All of them watched breathlessly as Billibonk's trunk inched cautiously through the thorns toward them. When it drew level with the first mice, almost touching them, Ragou whistled. The first two teams released the branches, which sprang together, trapping Billibonk's trunk. The third team set to work frantically splashing the stinking purple berries at the elephant's trunk. Seconds later, the job was done, and the mice again hauled the thorn branches apart to set the elephant free.

The elephant herd had stepped back in alarm while Billibonk struggled with the thorn bush. When he finally yanked his trunk free, they gasped. The end of his trunk had turned purple!

"He woke the Thorn Monster!" cried one elephant. Another yelled, "The monster's poisoned Billibonk!"

The panicked elephants wheeled around and stampeded, trumpeting as they escaped, but taking care to stay well away from thorn patches.

The elephant who ran the fastest didn't trumpet at all: Billibonk's trunk was too sore, and he could barely breathe, he was so terrified. "Why do I have the worst luck?" he moaned as he ran.

Back at the thorn patch, the mice laughed and laughed, and congratulated themselves on their cleverness. Their scheme had worked exactly as planned. They might not have been so happy, however, if they had realized what was happening above them. Up in the jungle canopy, a group of monkeys had begun chattering together about what they had seen and heard below.

Frankl Explains:

Why Billibonk had "bad luck" with the Thorn Monster.

Often, the problem you have today . . .

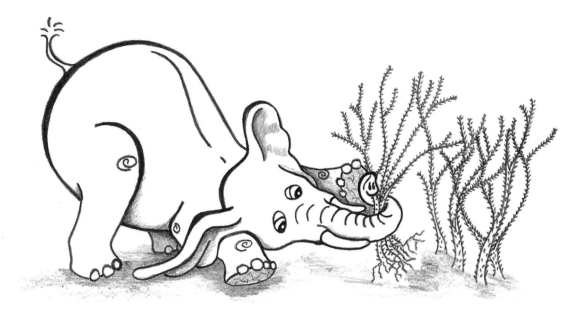

has happened because of the "great idea" you had for solving . . .

the problem you had yesterday.

Part Two

Monkey Business

Most animals treat monkeys with caution. Monkeys are obviously smart; some say as smart as mice. They are not nearly as patient as mice, though. They want to have everything without working for it. As a result, they are often cunning rather than clever.

As the monkeys watched the mice trick Billibonk and the rest of the elephant herd, they at once started scheming. "If mice can trick elephants, so can we. How can we get elephants to make our lives easier?"

In their chattering, the troop hit upon a plan that would involve some work but that would leave them with more time than ever for play and sleep—the two things monkeys enjoy most. The plan involved what monkeys call a "dupe"—a trick to get others to do what you want while thinking it is their idea. The job of duping an elephant was given to Chekup. With his roguish face and engaging smile, Chekup had proven his craftiness with hundreds of practical jokes on other monkeys. Chekup got to work. He secretly prepared a leafy yakka-yakka branch and then set off to find an elephant. Swinging through the branches of a large tree, he finally spotted Honka, who was casually strolling along a jungle path. Hanging by his tail, Chekup dangled the yakka-yakka branch in Honka's path. "Hey, elephant!" he yelled, "Look at this!"

Honka halted. "That's a nice-looking branch," he said, and he smacked his lips.

"This is more than nice," said Chekup. "You try these leaves. They're special."

"Don't mind if I do," said Honka, and he folded the leaves into his mouth. Soon the branch was bare. "Those were *very* nice," agreed Honka. "Not as prickly as usual. In fact, I'd say they were the smoothest and nicest yakka-yakka I've ever eaten."

"Want to know why?" asked Chekup.

"I sure would," said Honka.

"Well, yakka-yakka are normally prickly because of these." He opened his hand to reveal a pile of hard yakka-yakka seeds. "These seeds grow among the leaves—I don't know how you elephants can stand crunching on them!"

"Hmmm. . .," mused Honka, who had never thought that yakka-yakka could taste any different.

"Of course, elephants can't take the seeds out," said Chekup, "because they don't have any thumbs. But monkeys can. In fact, we're the only animals in the jungle with the thumbs to do it."

"Wow!" said Honka. "Could you take the seeds out for us elephants?"

"I hadn't thought of that," lied Chekup. "I guess if we monkeys worked together we could, but it would be a lot of hard work. We may not have enough time to get our own food."

"I have an idea," said Honka. "I can get the herd to bring yakka-yakka branches to you, and we can bring some of your food, too. What do monkeys eat, anyway?"

"You're brilliant, elephant!" said Chekup. "We eat any kind of fruit, like those bananas over there. You can get fruit anywhere in the jungle; there's plenty just around here. Let's meet back here in an hour. You bring the fruit and the yakka-yakka leaves, and I'll have some monkeys ready to get rid of the seeds. Is it a deal?"

"Right," said Honka, and he galloped off to tell the herd of their great opportunity.

The other elephants jostled each other excitedly at the thought of a new taste sensation. "At last, some good luck," they crowed, as they headed off to

23

collect
the
yakka-yakka
branches and
fruit. They had no trouble   gathering a good quantity
near the arranged meeting place.   When the monkeys arrived,
the elephants eagerly waited to get their first taste of seedless yakka-yakka.

The monkey troop swarmed over the yakka-yakka to remove the seeds.
They were not too fussy, however. They had decided that elephants were so
used to eating the seeds that they would not notice a few left behind. In just a
few minutes, they had finished the task.

"There you go, elephant," said Chekup, as he peeled the skin off a banana
and lay back against a comfortable rock. "Next time, though, I think we'll need
a bit more fruit."

"Sorry," said Honka. "I didn't realize how many monkeys it took to get the
seeds out." He took another mouthful of the delicious, seed-free yakka-yakka,
and decided that this new treat was worth all the effort.

"Oh yes," said Chekup. "It takes a lot of monkeys—it's very hard work, you
know, finding such small seeds."

"I imagine it is," said Honka. Then, realizing the yakka-yakka was almost
gone, he added, "If I go and get some more leaves—and some more fruit, of
course—will you still be here when I get back?"

"Sure," said Chekup, as he peeled another banana. "We can do that for you,
no trouble."

CHAPTER SEVEN
Elephant Dung

Over the next week, Frankl watched sadly as the elephants ran back and forth, collecting yakka-yakka branches and fruit for the monkeys. Each day the elephants had to go farther afield to collect the fruit, and each day they had less time to enjoy their seed-free leaves.

The other mice just laughed at the elephants. In their opinion, this was the elephant herd's problem and had nothing to do with them. But Frankl disagreed. If something was bad for one animal, he reasoned, one day it would be bad for the whole jungle. Frankl had seen that animals of all sorts depended on one another—often without realizing it. He decided to do what he could to help the elephants.

That day Frankl scurried over to an elephant slumped under a shady tree, recovering from a busy morning of fruit gathering. "Hey, elephant. You're Billibonk, aren't you?"

Billibonk opened his weary eyes, spotted Frankl, and said, "Yes, I am. Aren't you the mouse who helped me out of the thorn patch?"

"Yes, my name's Frankl. You had a problem then, and now *all* the elephants have a problem: they're doing business with the monkeys."

"Oh," said Billibonk. "Why is that a problem?"

"Let me show you," said Frankl, "You won't have to go far."

Billibonk lumbered to his feet and followed Frankl a short way through the jungle. They came upon an old pile of elephant dung. "Do you know what this is?" asked Frankl.

"Of course I know what it is," harrumphed Billibonk. "I suppose you mice don't make dung."

"All animals make dung," said Frankl. "It's quite a normal thing to do. But, do you notice anything unusual about this pile?"

Billibonk had never really given much attention to old piles of dung, so he looked closer. "There seems to be something growing up out of it."

"Yes," said Frankl. "That's a baby yakka-yakka tree."

"Really?" said Billibonk, looking closer. He could make out the distinctive shape of the leaves, even though the shoot was tiny. "You're right! How did that get in there?"

"Everything in the jungle is good for something," explained Frankl, "and dung is especially good for making things grow. This dung is helping the baby yakka-yakka to grow. Yakka-yakka trees start out as seeds—the ones that are in the leaves."

"Oh," said Billibonk, "so the seeds fall off the trees, land in dung, and start to grow."

"No," said Frankl, to Billibonk's surprise. "That could happen, I suppose, but usually it doesn't. What happens is that you elephants eat the seeds along with the leaves. The seeds go all the way through your body and come out, ready to grow."

"That's amazing!" said Billibonk, as he started to realize the importance of what Frankl was saying. "But the monkeys are taking the seeds out of the yakka-yakka leaves. Is that a problem?"

"Well, it may mean that after a while there will be no new yakka-yakka trees."

"What if we collected seeds and put them into piles of dung?" asked Billibonk, hopefully.

"Well, it isn't a job I'd like to do," said Frankl, "and I've never seen yakka-yakka seeds growing in any other way. So I think a seed probably has to go right through an elephant before it's ready to sprout into a tree."

Billibonk thought about this for some time. He thought about the taste of seed-free yakka-yakka, and he thought about having no yakka-yakka at all. "How long would it take before we ran out of yakka-yakka? There seems to be plenty in the forest."

"It depends," said Frankl, "on how long the trees take to grow. Throughout the jungle, there are yakka-yakka of all sizes. They'll probably keep you fed for a long time. But one day there won't be any left."

At the thought of this, Billibonk felt quite light-headed. Ever since he could remember, yakka-yakka had always been there when he was hungry. He did not know how long it took to grow. He did not even know how long elephants lived—it seemed to be a long time. Yet the jungle could run out of yakka-yakka at any moment—almost certainly during his own lifetime.[8] "We have to do something!" he blurted out.

Frankl was amazed that an elephant could be so easy to teach. "The first thing to do," he said "is to start eating the seeds again. And start talking about this to the other elephants, too. They're not being very clever about this. See if

you can get some others to understand why the seeds are important."

"I think elephants can be as clever as anyone else," said Billibonk. "This has just been bad luck really. But what if some of the herd won't listen?"

"I don't think you'll have a problem. Monkeys often have trouble keeping

---

[8] Although Billibonk did not know the time involved, he was right in thinking they would run out of trees in his lifetime. Elephants generally live about 60 years (Billibonk was 23 years old), and yakka-yakka trees take 20 years to mature.

their schemes working. Each time one more elephant stops bringing fruit to the monkeys, it'll be harder for the rest of the herd to keep going. But Billibonk, I want you to think about something. Is it really 'bad luck' when you get *yourself* into trouble?" And with that he scuttled off, very pleased with himself.

Elephants Can Learn

illibonk was enjoying a relaxed feed of yakka-yakka, seeds and all. He found that he liked the prickly seeds, knowing that eating them meant there would be more to eat when he was older. He still wondered how he could persuade the rest of the herd to go back to eating the seeds. After all, he was the only one who knew how important the seeds were.

Billibonk's friend Cody came trotting by, on his way to gather more fruit and yakka-yakka. Cody was dark-eyed and handsome, with long, elegant tusks and only a few facial whiskers. He stopped when he saw Billibonk. "Why are you eating yakka-yakka with the seeds still in it?" he asked.

"I'm glad you asked," said Billibonk eagerly, and he told Cody how yakka-yakka grew. "Actually," he concluded, "I also enjoy not having to run around all day finding fruit for those monkeys!"

This made good sense to Cody, and he happily started eating the yakka-yakka with Billibonk. Later that day, both he and Billibonk talked to several other elephants about how yakka-yakka grew. More and more elephants began talking about the importance of seeds. Some, like Honka, were determined never to eat seeds again, but many decided to go back to the "old-fashioned" way.

Fewer and fewer elephants were now eating the seedless yakka-yakka, but more and more monkeys wanted to keep taking the seeds out in return for fruit. Monkeys had come from all over the jungle to enjoy the cheap meal the elephants were providing. Now there was not enough fruit to keep them all happy.

Whenever an elephant returned with trunkloads of fruit, fights broke out among the monkeys over who should get it. Those who missed out screeched at the elephant to work harder, run faster, and carry more.

After two days of arguing, even Honka decided that nothing was worth this much trouble. The seed-free yakka-yakka business was finished....

Meanwhile, Billibonk was spending a lot of time thinking. He found that he enjoyed thinking about how the jungle worked. It amazed him how everything had a use—even dung.

One night he also thought about "bad luck." Was it true what Frankl had said? Did elephants get *themselves* into trouble?

At first he resisted the idea that problems were often his own fault. But then he had a thought. It was a great thought. He was so pleased with the thought that a delighted little "toot" escaped from his trunk. His thought was: "Sometimes animals are so busy finding someone else to blame, or blaming bad luck, that they don't do anything about the problem. If a problem is my fault, then maybe I can fix it. I might even figure out how to avoid problems in the first place."

Delighted at the idea of no more "bad luck," Billibonk started musing about the things that had happened to him. Could he have stopped them from happening?

He thought first about sitting on the thorns. How did he walk into the patch? It was because he was looking up instead of watching where he was going. To check his theory, he found a thorn patch and practiced walking around it looking at the ground and then up at the trees. After a while, he found that he could do it! "No more walking into thorn patches for me!" he trumpeted.

But what about his bad luck with the Thorn Monster? He stared for a while at the thorn patch. Then he remembered that, at first, he had not believed there were any Thorn Monsters. He had lived in the jungle for 23 years without ever hearing about them. And nothing had grabbed him when he was sitting crying in the thorns.

Billibonk noticed a gap in his practice thorn patch. Carefully, and nervously, he poked his trunk into the gap. Farther and farther his trunk went in. Nothing happened. Nothing at all. "Those mice tricked us," he realized, "so we wouldn't pull up their homes. The crafty little short-snouts!"

Billibonk turned and trotted off to join the elephant herd at the watering hole. He had a lot to tell them. And already a plan was forming in his head; a plan that would show those mice that elephants *could* learn.

Frankl Explains:

Why the monkey business went bust.

Sometimes, because everyone demands a share . . .

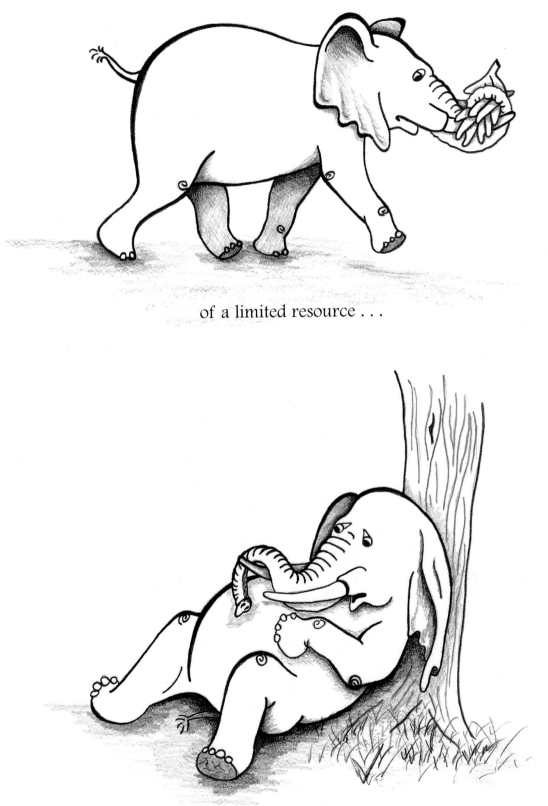

of a limited resource . . .

the resource gives out.

Part Three

A Lesson for Mice

t was a warm, quiet evening in the jungle. As the elephant herd lolled peacefully on the banks of the swimming hole, Billibonk announced, "I put my trunk in a thorn patch today."

"But what about the Thorn Monster?" asked Cody. "I know you have a lot of bad luck, but that's just asking for trouble!"

"Actually, *nothing* happened," said Billibonk. "Nothing happened because there *is* no Thorn Monster." The herd gasped in amazement. Billibonk explained, "That was just a trick by the mice to stop us from pulling up the thorns."

"Why would they do that?" asked Jawoody.

"Because," said Billibonk, "they live in the thorns. They didn't want us wrecking their homes."

"Well, that makes my trunk curl," said Honka. "We should teach those short-snouts a lesson. Let's pull up a thorn patch."

"I thought about that," said Billibonk, not wanting to be rude to Honka, "and the way I figure it, we probably shouldn't hurt other animals, especially little ones. After all, they were just trying to protect their homes. But, I do think we should teach them a lesson. And I have an idea."

The elephants had to concentrate hard as they listened to Billibonk's plan. They furrowed their brows, and scratched their heads with their trunks. And, one by one, they understood his plan.

"I like this idea," said Jawoody. "It's

just what those mice deserve. But what if they don't fall for it?"

"This trick is to teach them a lesson," said Billibonk, "and I really think it'll work."

"Why?" asked Cody.

"Because they seem to be thinking they're cleverer than they really are."

The next morning the plan went into operation. Like most elephant ideas, it was very simple. The elephants just had to get it going, and the mice would do the rest.

Cody, who loved to act, wanted to be the first one to approach the mice. The rest of the herd appreciated Cody's talent and agreed that he was perfect for this role. He and Billibonk practiced just what he would say. Then they went out to look for a mouse.

Even for those elephants who bother to look, all mice appear much the same. So it was quite by accident that the mouse they came upon first was Yollanda. They were in luck: Yollanda was just the sort of mouse they needed for the plan to work—she was a "know-it-all" with a very low opinion of elephants.

"Hey, mouse," called Cody, taking care not to be too loud for the little creature's small ears. "Can you tell us some more about the Thorn Monster? We're afraid of it and don't want to upset it again."

Yollanda grinned. "Sure, elephant. What do you want to know?"

"Is it true that you dance and give flowers to the Thorn Monster during a full moon?"

"That's right," said Yollanda, remembering what Nettie had explained when they gave the elephants the great fright. "We dance and sing. It's a great time. The Thorn Monster enjoys it too."

"Does the Thorn Monster come out of the thorns?" asked Cody.

"Sometimes, but not very often," replied Yollanda, cautiously.

"There will be a full moon in three nights, won't there? I suppose all the mice are excited."

"Yes," said Yollanda, rather nervously. She had not thought of when the next full moon would be.

"We'd love to join the celebration," said Cody. "We've never seen a Thorn Monster dance before, and *we* want to keep the Thorn Monster happy, too."

"I'm not sure about that," said Yollanda. "You have to be careful with Thorn Monsters."

"Look," said Cody, "we would be *very* quiet. We'd stay right out of the way. And we could bring flowers, too. You tell us where the dance will be, and we'll be there."

"I really should talk to the other mice about this," said Yollanda.

"All right," said Cody. "Let's meet here at the same time tomorrow, and you can tell me what they said. This'll be great fun!" And with that, he and Billibonk turned and trotted away, smiling at one another.

Getting Ready

News of Yollanda's talk with Cody spread quickly among the mice. Another meeting of the Mouse Council was called for the very next morning.

Ragou opened the meeting. "We're here to talk about elephants and Thorn Monsters again. It seems that those pachycraniums want to join us for a Thorn Monster celebration." The assembled mice burst out laughing and chattered to one another once more about the "Great Fright."

Ragou called for quiet, and then continued, "Well then, what shall we do?"

Frankl stood up. "I never liked the Thorn Monster idea," he began. "I think elephants are much smarter than we say they are."

"Oh, come on, Frankl!" said Yollanda. "The Thorn Monster fright worked perfectly. It saved our homes. Anyway, what do you think we should do?"

"I think we should tell the elephants the truth: that there is no Thorn Monster. We should tell them that it was all a trick to save our homes."

"I don't believe it!" Yollanda exclaimed. "We can't do that. We'd all look like idiots. And Nettie and I have both told them that Thorn Monsters *do* exist. I don't want the elephants thinking I'm a liar!"

"If you don't want to be called a liar," Frankl thought to himself, "then you shouldn't tell lies!" But he decided not to say what he was thinking; Nettie and Yollanda looked angry, and the rest of the mice seemed to be siding with them.[9]

"We've already decided to trick the elephants about this," said Nettie. "We can't go changing our minds now. If we told them the truth, they might want to pull up the thorn bushes again. Even one mad elephant could destroy the homes of a thousand mice!"

"If we're all agreed, then," said Ragou, "let's start planning what we'll do tomorrow night."

Frankl, who did not agree at all, shook his head sadly and quietly left the chamber. While some noticed him go, no one tried to stop him. They had

---

[9] Of course, Frankl would never know how angry they really were, because he did not ask them.

heard enough from Frankl that night.

The next day, as arranged, Yollanda met with Billibonk and Cody. Excitedly, she announced that the elephants were invited to attend the Thorn Monster celebration the following night. "We start as soon as it is dark," explained Yollanda, "in the clearing where you first met the Thorn Monster."

"We'll be there," said Cody. "The whole herd is looking forward to it."

And off they all went to prepare. Yollanda, along with a group of other mice, made strings of flowers, the gifts for the Thorn Monster. The rest of the mice practiced the songs and dances they had arranged.

Billibonk and Cody prepared in quite a different way. After telling the rest of the herd of the arrangements, they began talking with as many other animals they could find: birds, buffalo, monkeys. They chatted with animals of all sorts, and they made a special effort

to seek out Chekup the monkey. They spread the word that everyone should come to the clearing the next evening for the best entertainment the jungle had ever seen.

CHAPTER ELEVEN

Mouse Dance

s the sun slowly set the next evening, elephants and other animals began gathering in groups at the clearing. All day the jungle had been buzzing with talk about the festival, and excitement filled the air. Frankl had decided not to take part in the mouse activities. He still thought that the evening was a mistake. "We should be helping them to be smarter, not trying to fool them any more," he complained to himself.

But Frankl—always the curious mouse—still wanted to see how everything would turn out. He found an observation point on the branch of a tall tree, overhanging the clearing. A number of other mice had positioned themselves in the branches around him. From these vantage points, they planned to play their part in the festivities. They did not mind Frankl sitting up in the tree with them, they told him, as long as he stayed quiet and kept out of their way.

When the elephants began crowding into the clearing, the mice grew tense. Some animals get very noisy when they are excited. Everyone knows when an elephant is agitated, for instance; the trumpeting blares throughout the jungle. Mice, however, have great difficulty being loud. When they are excited, they energetically brush and groom their whiskers and fur. The mice waiting around Frankl were quickly becoming the cleanest mice in the history of the jungle.

Frankl noticed other animals besides elephants gathering at the clearing. "What's going on?" he wondered. Some of the other mice had noticed as well and were holding whispered conversations. One youngster scurried over to a more experienced mouse close to Frankl and asked, "Should I go and tell Ragou?"

"It's too late, now," whispered back the older mouse. "We're about to start. Don't worry, I'm sure Ragou has everything under control."

Darkness had fallen, and moonlight bathed the clearing. Ragou gave the sign for the performance to begin, believing that everything was going just as the mice had planned.

At Ragou's signal, mice in the trees above the clearing began dropping pink and white flower petals down into the clearing. As the petals fluttered down like snowflakes, the onlookers gave a sigh of appreciation. It was unlike anything they had ever seen before—probably because it never snows in Knith.

The petals showered down more thickly now, and dozens of mice danced into the clearing. They formed two great circles, and began singing.

> O *Thorn Monster, Thorn Monster,*
> *Clever and strong,*
> O *Thorn Monster, Thorn Monster,*
> *Please hear our song.*
> *You make the thorns a place of charm,*
> *by everything you do.*
> *You keep us safe and free from harm*
> *and keep us happy, too.*

Suddenly, the center of the thorn patch began to rustle. The mice paused, puzzled, and stared at each other in confusion.

To everyone's amazement, a shadowy figure, bristling with thorns and twisting madly, burst from the patch. As the horrified onlookers watched, the grotesque creature leapt from the patch into the clearing, howling, "BOOOOOOOoooooooooh!"

The mice shrieked with fright. Several fainted. "There *is* a Thorn Monster!" yelled one. A young mouse cried to his mother, "You *told* me the Thorn Monster was just make-believe!"

All around the clearing, the animals trembled at the sight of the thorny beast. Finally, Billibonk spoke up. "Look, everyone. It's just Chekup, the monkey."

The animals gaped in disbelief as the dark creature began plucking off the thorns stuck to its body. It *was* Chekup. Billibonk had promised him three bunches of the best bananas in the jungle for his Thorn Monster performance.

The elephants began to chortle at the shocked expressions on the faces of the mice. Cody called out, "What's wrong, mice? Weren't you *expecting* a Thorn Monster?"

Chekup puffed out his chest proudly. He danced around the clearing, laughing and explaining to anyone who would listen how the mice had been scared by a monster *they* had invented to scare elephants.

"Oh, no," said Frankl to himself, high in the tree.

"How humiliating," said Ragou, from the edge of the thorn patch.

"Let's get out of here!" yelled Yollanda, from the circle of dancers. And as the other animals roared with laughter, the blushing mice scurried off into the night.

"Hey, bad luck mice!" Honka called after them.

Frankl Explains:

Why the mice fell for the elephants' trick.

When you think you're better than everyone else . . .

others work harder to prove you're not . . .

and you're in for a surprise.

Part Four

CHAPTER TWELVE

What Next?

he animals around the clearing slowly dispersed, many still chuckling. Some of them called out, "Hey, elephants! That was great!"

The elephant herd relaxed in the center of the clearing, enjoying the warm glow of success. This was something unusual for them; they were much more used to having "bad luck." Success felt much, much better.

Chekup danced over: he had run out of other animals to whom he could brag about his marvelous acting. "That was so much fun!" he screeched. "We should start planning our next trick. In fact, next time you want me to help out, I'll do it for nothing!"[10]

As Chekup left, Honka breathed a contented sigh. "Wow," he said. "Even the monkeys thought our trick was great. We must really be good at this. There's a lot to be said for this thinking business."

The other elephants nodded and grinned. Cody said, "Let's think up another lesson we could teach those mice!"

Frankl was still hidden on his branch above the clearing. Hearing the elephants talk about more tricks made him very nervous, and he began anxiously cleaning his whiskers. But Frankl gave a quiet "Whew!" of relief when he heard Billibonk say to the herd: "It *was* fun making this trick work. And we *were* good at it! But, I'm not sure . . . another one might cause trouble."

"What do you mean?" asked Jawoody. She was coming to respect Billibonk's opinion more and more.

"Well," replied Billibonk, "those monkeys were good at taking the seeds out of yakka-yakka, but that didn't make it a good thing to do. In fact, it was a bad thing, really. It just made our lives miserable running all over the jungle. And eventually we would have run out of food. I don't think we should do something just because we're good at it."

"We could do it just for fun," suggested Cody.

Billibonk thought about this for a while. As he mulled it over, Frankl scuttled nervously back and forth along the branch above the elephants. He could

---

[10] Some of the elephants noticed that Chekup was taking much of the credit for himself, even though they had planned the whole trick, but they did not want to spoil the moment by starting an argument with him.

imagine all sorts of problems for mice and other animals if elephants started regularly playing tricks around the jungle.

"It's true," Billibonk said at last. "We *could* do things just for fun. But what if something goes wrong? If we played another trick on the mice, for instance, they could decide to get back at us again."

"Oh sure," snorted Honka. "What could a mouse do to me? Bite me on the toenail?" The herd chortled.

When they finally quieted down again, Billibonk said, "We almost got into big trouble because of little yakka-yakka seeds and a little trick. Maybe enough little things all together can make a big problem."

With a heave, Jawoody pushed herself to her full height, commanding everyone's attention. "I don't really understand what big problems could come along," she announced, "but I think Billibonk is being sensible. We haven't been doing enough of this thinking and tricking to know what can happen. We've taught those short-snout mice a lesson; let's be happy with that. I say it's time for some sleep, then a good bath in the river." Amid a rumble of agreement from the others, she hefted herself into a comfortable space and nestled down for a nap.

The herd quickly followed her example. All the talking and thinking had made them tired.[11]

Billibonk, too, had begun to doze off when he heard a quiet "plop" beside his head. He opened one eye to find Frankl standing in front of him. "I'm sorry, elephant," said the mouse. "But I don't think you should go off to sleep just yet. There's still work for you to do, I'm afraid. Follow me."

---

[11] The herd was discovering that thinking is hard work, especially for animals unused to it.

Planning

Billibonk did his best to tiptoe as he followed Frankl down one of the paths leading away from the clearing, until they could talk without disturbing the slumbering herd. "What's the problem, mouse?" Billibonk asked. "I hope you're not too upset about our trick."

"It was very upsetting at first," admitted Frankl. "I don't mind telling you, it is hugely embarrassing for a mouse to be tricked by any other animal. But the more I think about it, the happier I feel."

"Oh!" said Billibonk, surprised. "Why is that?"

"It's hard to explain," said Frankl. "You see, we mice decided to fool you elephants with the Thorn Monster story because we thought you couldn't learn about how the small parts of the jungle work.[12] But when I heard you talking to the other elephants just now, I realized that you've been learning plenty. In fact, you've started to teach *me* things."

Billibonk blushed the full length of his trunk. "Thanks, Frankl . . . but, what's still to be done?"

Frankl shuffled nervously. "I think the other mice might already be plan-

ning some way of getting even with you elephants. We've got to stop them."

"Why do you need me? They'll listen to you, won't they?"

Frankl squirmed, hating to admit the mice's bad behavior and his failure to change their thinking. "I don't think they'll listen to me at the moment. And they'll lis-

ten to you only if I introduce you as my friend. We'll have to work together."

---

[12] Billibonk was impressed at Frankl's openness. It would have been easy for Frankl to blame the other mice, but he did not.

CHAPTER THIRTEEN

"You know, Frankl, I'd like to work together with you. I always feel good after we talk. We should keep doing it!" Frankl grinned happily. "But first I need some sleep," Billibonk said pleadingly. "My head feels like it's going to fall off. Have I got time for a nap?"

"I guess so," said Frankl. "Mouse Council meetings usually start just after sunrise, which doesn't give you very long."

"What if I can't wake up in time?" groaned Billibonk, his brow furrowing.

"Don't worry about that," Frankl said, with a mischievous grin. "I won't be sleeping, and I know of a way to wake you up."

Can Mice Learn?

The mice were still shame-faced when they came together early that morning for a Mouse Council meeting.

"Yesterday was the worst day for mice in the history of the jungle," said Ragou sadly.

"I *knew* we should have listened to Frankl," muttered an older mouse.

"Well, we didn't," said Ragou, "and it's too late now to change what happened. Anyway, where is Frankl?"

Yollanda spoke up in a grumpy voice. "He's probably off somewhere practicing how to say 'I told you so.'"

"We don't need to be mad at Frankl," said Ragou. "He just tried to stop us from getting into trouble. It's the elephants who made us look silly."

Mice do not like looking foolish, so they were all happy to blame the elephants for their problems. "What can we do to get back at them?" asked Yollanda.

"I don't think we should do anything too nasty," stammered Bekk.

"Why not?" protested Yollanda. "After all, they started it."

The mice all paused for a moment, thinking about how they might exact revenge. Before they could say anything else, however, a yell came from above them. As they stared in amazement, a mouse came swinging down toward them through a hole in the thorns, hanging onto the end of a long, gray object.

"It's Frankl!" said Ragou. "What's that you're riding, Frankl?"

"This," said Frankl proudly, "is part of a very large friend of mine—Billibonk—he's an elephant, you know."

"You're friends with an elephant?" gasped Ragou.

"Billibonk and I have been talking, and we find we have a lot in common," Frankl declared, as he jumped to the ground. He banged twice on the end of Billibonk's trunk, and it disappeared back up through the gap in the thorns. "Billibonk would like to talk to us all. Let's go out into the clearing."

"He won't hurt us, will he?" asked Bekk.

"No," said Frankl. "He's very friendly. Honest!"

"OK," said Ragou. "Let's hear what he has to say." He went out through the thorns to where Billibonk stood. The rest of the mice followed close behind.

"Hey, mice," said Billibonk. He was feeling refreshed from his sleep, though

the tip of his tail still throbbed slightly from the bite Frankl had used to wake him up. He made a mental note to tell Honka to keep his opinions about small animals to himself.

Coming to the point, Billibonk said, "I guess you're all feeling pretty mad at us elephants after yesterday. But can't we find a way to get along together?"

"Why should we listen to you, after what you did to us?" asked Ragou.

"I don't blame you for asking that," said Billibonk. "We were mad at you mice when we found out you had tricked us about the Thorn Monster, so I know how you probably feel about us. You might even want to do something to get back at us." When Billibonk saw how the mice began to blush and clean their whiskers, he knew he had guessed right.

Yollanda was not convinced. "How do we know this isn't another trick?" she shouted to the mice. "Maybe he just wants to confuse us while the elephants get ready to fool us again."

"Look. This is no trick!" Frankl interjected. "I listened to the elephants talking. They don't want any more trouble."

"That's true," said Billibonk. "We've had enough. But if you mice do something to us," he continued, "we'll probably want to do something else to get back at you. Then you would want to get back at us, and on and on. Unless we sort this out, things could get dangerous for mice *and* elephants—and probably for the other animals, too."

"What do you mean?" asked Ragou.

"Well, when those monkeys saw you trick us, they decided that they could fool us, too. If we start fighting and getting revenge on each other, all sorts of animals could decide to copy us, and the problem will just keep getting bigger," Billibonk explained.

The listening mice realized that Billibonk was right. "He's starting to think like a mouse," whispered Nettie to Yollanda, who nodded in grudging agreement.[13]

"Every now and then," Billibonk said, "we'll make each other mad. But we all live in the same jungle, and so we need to think of other animals, too."

Mice all around the clearing began nodding and clapping. Some of the braver mice, including Yollanda, hopped over and patted Billibonk on the trunk. "You've reminded us of an important lesson," Yollanda said. "Thank you, elephant."

"I think yesterday may end up being the best day for mice in the history of the jungle," thought Frankl to himself.

---

[13] Fortunately, Billibonk did not hear Nettie's remark. Although a mouse would consider this an enormous compliment, elephants are happy to think like elephants. Mice sometimes have trouble understanding that other animals do not necessarily want to be just like them.

Satisfaction

Billibonk lounged in the shade of a tall, leafy tree. Despite the early hour, the day was already hot. Frankl perched on Billibonk's shoulder, close to the elephant's huge ear. They had not talked much since the meeting with the Mouse Council. They were happy just to sit together and reflect on the events of the past few days.

Eventually Billibonk stirred. "I'd better get moving. The herd will be at the swimming hole soon, and I need to have some breakfast before my bath. It's been good knowing you, Frankl."

"But you make it sound like we won't see each other again," said Frankl.

"Well, that might happen," said Billibonk, a sad tone entering his voice. His eyes and trunk began to run. "After all, I spent a long time in this jungle without ever seeing you, or any mouse."

Frankl thought about this briefly, and then smiled. "Oh, don't be ridiculous. You didn't see us mice because you weren't looking. We've been here all along, you know. Now that you know I exist, I'll bet you'll be surprised how often we meet."

Billibonk looked startled for a moment, and then he laughed. "I guess you're right. Let's make *sure* we stay friends. I like talking with you, Frankl—you sure know a lot!"

"You do, too, you know," said Frankl shyly. "I've learned a lot from *you*."

"Like what?" asked Billibonk, surprised that he had taught the mouse something.

"Listening to you, I've learned the difference between being clever and being wise," Frankl replied. "The Thorn Monster trick was clever, but it wasn't wise. It just got us mice into more trouble."

"I get it!" said Billibonk. "Being wise means doing what is best in the long run."

"That's it," said Frankl. "Though, sometimes it takes a while to realize what *is* best—you have to know the jungle and the different animals in it, and that takes time. In fact, you never really finish learning. And, you always learn more when you learn together with someone else."

"That's so true," said Billibonk with an enthusiastic nod. After a pause, he said, "Well, Frankl, see you soon, I hope." He lifted Frankl to the ground with his trunk and trotted off. This time, his gaze moved back and forth from tree-tops to ground as he looked for yakka-yakka *and* carefully avoided thorns.

Frankl watched him go and chuckled to himself. "His luck has certainly changed," he said with a smile.

Frankl Explains:

Why helping elephants learn is better than tricking them.

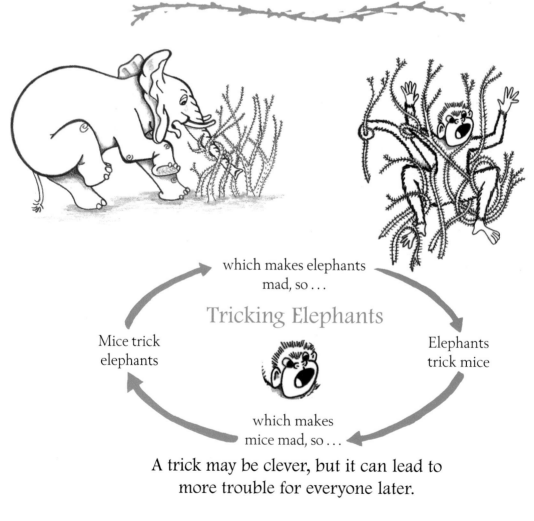

which makes elephants
mad, so . . .

Tricking Elephants

Mice trick
elephants

Elephants
trick mice

which makes
mice mad, so . . .

A trick may be clever, but it can lead to
more trouble for everyone later.

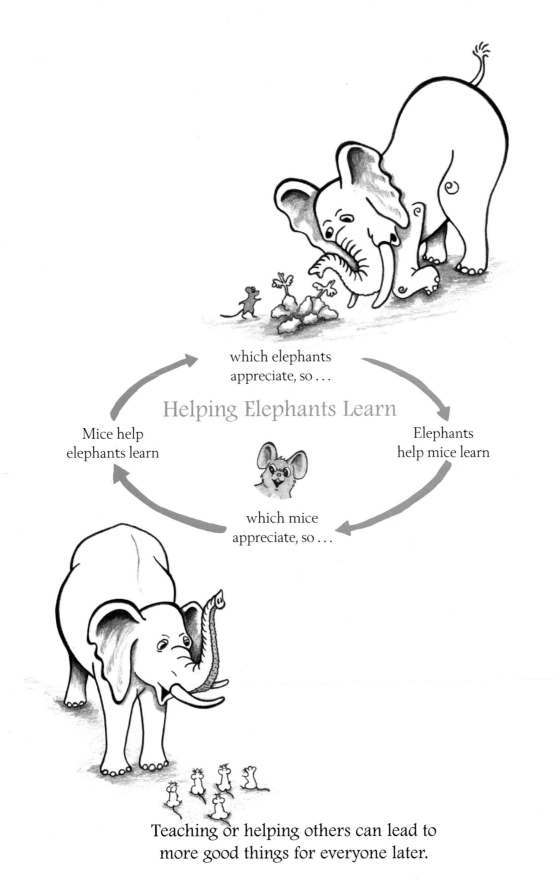

which elephants
appreciate, so . . .

Helping Elephants Learn

Mice help
elephants learn

Elephants
help mice learn

which mice
appreciate, so . . .

Teaching or helping others can lead to
more good things for everyone later.

Acknowledgments (for Children)

Writing a story like this is both fun and hard work. I needed help to get it written, and then more help to fix all the mistakes. The people who helped me to write this were:
· my kids, Alex and Nick, who made sure I had plenty of ideas to work with
· my wife, Debbie, who told me when my ideas didn't work, and helped me fix my spelling
· my editors, Laurie and Kellie, who made sure the story was easy to read
· Robin and her mom, Madaleen, who illustrated the book so brilliantly.

If you want to write a book, you have to find people who will point out your mistakes. They have to be smart enough to see the mistakes you can't, and they have to care enough to be fussy. It was great that these people were very smart, and very caring.

Acknowledgments (for Adults)

While I hope that adults will read, enjoy, and learn from this book, it really is for children. Writing for children now seems very normal, yet several years ago I would not have imagined myself doing so. What changed?

Some time ago, a friend of mine, Mike Bebb, suggested that I write a novel about a learning organization. I dismissed the thought as one of Mike's nuttier ideas: I wasn't a novelist, and I certainly didn't feel I knew enough about organizational learning to do justice to the topic.

There were at least two flawed assumptions in my thinking. First, I assumed that you become a novelist and then write novels; second, that you learn so that you can write. My son Nicholas, then six, helped me get started writing anyway. We got into an impossible impasse one night, over his refusal to eat his dinner. The more Debbie and I insisted, the more upset he became, and the more determined we became that his emotions weren't going to govern what we ate! We got completely stuck in the conflict, much like an elephant stuck in a thorn patch. I made up a story as a way out of our stuckness—and it worked! It occurred to me that stories are a great way to help kids see beyond their immediate feelings, and look at the underlying structure of their problems. I liked the idea of parents being able to say to their children, "You know, this seems a lot like the time when Billibonk . . ." It also occurred to me that our story would make a good first chapter of a book, so I set about writing the rest.

Just like that, I discovered that writing a novel makes one a novelist. I also found out that writing helps learning. Creating the story forced me to integrate ideas from

64

people whose work I have admired; people like Peter Senge, Chris Argyris, Peter Block, Ian Mitroff, and Robert Fritz.

Whereas Nick helped me get the book started, my daughter Alexandra made sure it was finished. Being two years older than Nick, Alex was an independent reader, and insisted on being first to see each chapter as soon as it was completed.

Before the book could get to print, a huge amount of editing was required—far more than I imagined when I began. My wife, Debbie, did a wonderful job in helping prepare the manuscript. Still, we were both amazed at the quality of the editorial help and support provided by Laurie Johnson and Kellie Wardman O'Reilly at Pegasus Communications.

Finally, I'm grateful to the following readers who reviewed the book and made many helpful suggestions: Alberto Bazzan, IBM-Europe; Bruno Bagnaschi, The Torrington Company; David Berdish, Ford Motor Company-EFHD; Mark Downing, Du Pont; Brian Maxwell, Sandia National Laboratories; Patti Russell, Federal Express Corporation; and Mary Scheetz, The Waters Foundation.

To all those mentioned above, along with the students and colleagues at Massey University who have prodded me intellectually, go my heartfelt thanks.

Phil Ramsey
Palmerston North, New Zealand

About the Author

Phil Ramsey

has worked at Massey University in New Zealand for 12 years, teaching and conducting research in training and development and organizational learning. He is the author of the book *Successful On-the-Job Training* (Palmerston North, NZ: Dunmore Press, 1993). *Billibonk and the Thorn Patch* is Phil's first work of fiction.

Phil and his family live in Palmerston North, New Zealand. While they occasionally share their house with itinerant mice, sadly they don't know any elephants.

Department of Human Resource
   Management
Massey University, Private Bag 11222
Palmerston North, New Zealand
Phone (06) 350-4284; Fax (06) 350-5608
Email P.L.Ramsey@massey.ac.nz

*Human Dynamics: A New Framework for Understanding People
and Realizing the Potential in Our Organizations*

*Managing the Rapids: Stories from the Forefront of the
Learning Organization*

Reflections on Creating Learning Organizations

The Toolbox Reprint Series
Systems Archetypes I
Systems Archetypes II
Systems Thinking Tools: A User's Reference Guide

The Systems Thinker™ Newsletter

The Innovations in Management Series
From Mechanistic to Social Systemic Thinking
Applying Systems Archetypes
(Other titles forthcoming)

Pegasus Communications, Inc. is dedicated to helping organizations soar to new heights of excellence. By providing the forum and resources, Pegasus helps managers articulate, explore, and understand the challenges they face in the complex, changing business world. For information about *The Systems Thinker*™ Newsletter, the annual *Systems Thinking in Action*™ Conference, the *Power of Systems Thinking*™ Conference, or other publications that are part of *The Organizational Learning Resource Library*™ Catalog, contact:
Pegasus Communications, Inc.
P.O. Box 120 Kendall Square
Cambridge, MA 02142-0001 USA.
Phone: (617) 576-1231   Fax: (617) 576-3114